For Patrick—M.F.

LADYBIRD BOOKS, INC.
Auburn, Maine 04210 U.S.A.
© LADYBIRD BOOKS LTD 1992
Loughborough, Leicestershire, England

Printed in U.S.A.

The Birthday Party Prize

By Margo Finch
Illustrated by Steve Smallman

Ladybird Books

When Sarah arrived at Lucy's birthday party, the first thing she saw was a pile of colorfully wrapped packages. "Are those your presents, Lucy?" she asked.

"No," said Lucy, "those are prizes. Everyone who wins a game at this party will get a prize."

I'm going to win a prize today, Sarah promised herself. She could hardly wait for the games to begin.

"We're going to play drop-the-clothespins," announced Lucy's mother. "Who wants to be first?"

"I do!" said Sarah. Dropping five clothespins into a bottle didn't look difficult at all.

Sarah held her breath, aimed the first clothespin carefully, and let it go. It went straight into the bottle.

Hooray! Sarah thought, peeking at the pile of prizes.

But the second clothespin hit the top of the bottle—*plink!*—
and bounced onto the rug. Sarah aimed the rest as carefully as
she could, but it was no use. Not a single one went in.

She tried not to show she was disappointed. James got four clothespins into the bottle, and Sarah clapped politely when Lucy's mother declared him the winner.

I'm going to win the next game, whatever it is, Sarah told herself.

Next was pin-the-tail-on-the-donkey. Sarah was sure she could put the tail in the right spot. When her turn came, she was blindfolded and spun about.

As she made her way across the room, Sarah could imagine Lucy's mother saying, "The winner is Sarah!"

As she stuck the tail in place, Sarah heard giggles. With a cold feeling inside, she pulled off the blindfold. She hadn't even come close to the donkey picture. She had stuck her tail to the piano!

When Gregory stuck his tail to the telephone, everyone laughed—except Sarah. When Melissa pinned her tail to the donkey and Lucy's mother said, "Melissa wins," everyone cheered—except Sarah. She knew she should feel happy for Melissa, but she didn't.

Musical chairs was next. Lucy's mother played jolly march music on the piano while everyone walked around a row of chairs. Sarah managed to get a seat time after time as others dropped out, one by one.

Soon there were only two chairs left, and Sarah, Gregory, and Lucy marched round and round. Then the music stopped. Sarah scrambled for a chair, but Lucy and Gregory were already sitting down.

"I'm afraid you're out, Sarah," said Lucy's mother. Sarah
nodded and walked away, afraid she'd cry if she tried to speak.

On the next round, Lucy was left standing. "Gregory is the winner!" said Lucy's mother. But Sarah didn't care. If she wasn't the winner, it didn't matter who won.

Sarah hadn't won a single game. She wished the party would end so she could go home.

"Let's play hide-and-seek," said Lucy. James was "it," and he covered his eyes and started counting to one hundred. Sarah didn't feel much like playing, but she trudged up the stairs to find a place to hide.

Down the hall and around the corner she came to a door, and opened it. It was a linen cupboard. Making sure no one was in sight, Sarah slipped inside. *I hope they never find me,* she thought, settling in behind a pile of towels.

It was warm and dark and cozy in the cupboard. Sarah closed her eyes....

When she opened her eyes again, she didn't know where she was. Then she remembered. Lucy's birthday party. She'd fallen asleep in the linen cupboard!

What if the party was all over and everyone had gone?
What if it was the middle of the night?

But when Sarah rushed downstairs, the party was still going on. "Sarah, dear, where have you been?" asked Lucy's mother. "We've just finished giving out the prizes."

"Oh," said Sarah sadly. At least she hadn't had to watch the winners enjoying them.

"But where *were* you?" asked Lucy.

"Hiding," said Sarah.

"If Sarah was hiding and nobody found her," said Melissa, "doesn't that mean she won?"

"Yes, I suppose so," said Lucy's mother. "You really won, Sarah."

"I did?" Sarah couldn't believe it. She hadn't even been trying to win!

"I have a special prize for you," said Lucy's mother. She handed Sarah a package wrapped in striped paper, and said, just as Sarah had imagined, "The winner is...Sarah!"

She was so proud she thought she would burst. The others clapped and cheered as she opened her prize. It was a box of pretty note paper.

As she ate a big slice of Lucy's birthday cake, Sarah thought, *I'm going to write a note saying thank you for a wonderful time.* It had turned out to be a lovely party after all!